TOUGH TUG

BY **Margaret Read MacDonald**

ILLUSTRATED BY **Rob McClurkan**

two lions

WELD AND RIVET!
BUILD A TUG!

"Hey, workers, make me strong!
Use sturdy steel
so big waves can't break me!"

7/2018

SITKA, AK

ANACORTES, WA
*(where Tough Tug
was built)*

SEATTLE, WA

PRIME AND PAINT!
PAINT AND PRIME!

"I am RED! I love RED!
Don't forget my name . . .
TOUGH TUG!"

SLIDE AND SLIDE AND AND

"Launch day!
Here I come . . ."

"Hooray! I'm floating! This is fun!
Wait till those boats see what Tough Tug can do!"

FORWARD . . . REVERSE!

"Forward. Oops.
Forward. Good!"

FORWARD . . . REVERSE!

"Now backward.
No! Look out behind."

SPEED AND STOP.
SPEED AND STOP.

"Hey, watch me speed!
Oh no! Oh no! . . . can't stop!"

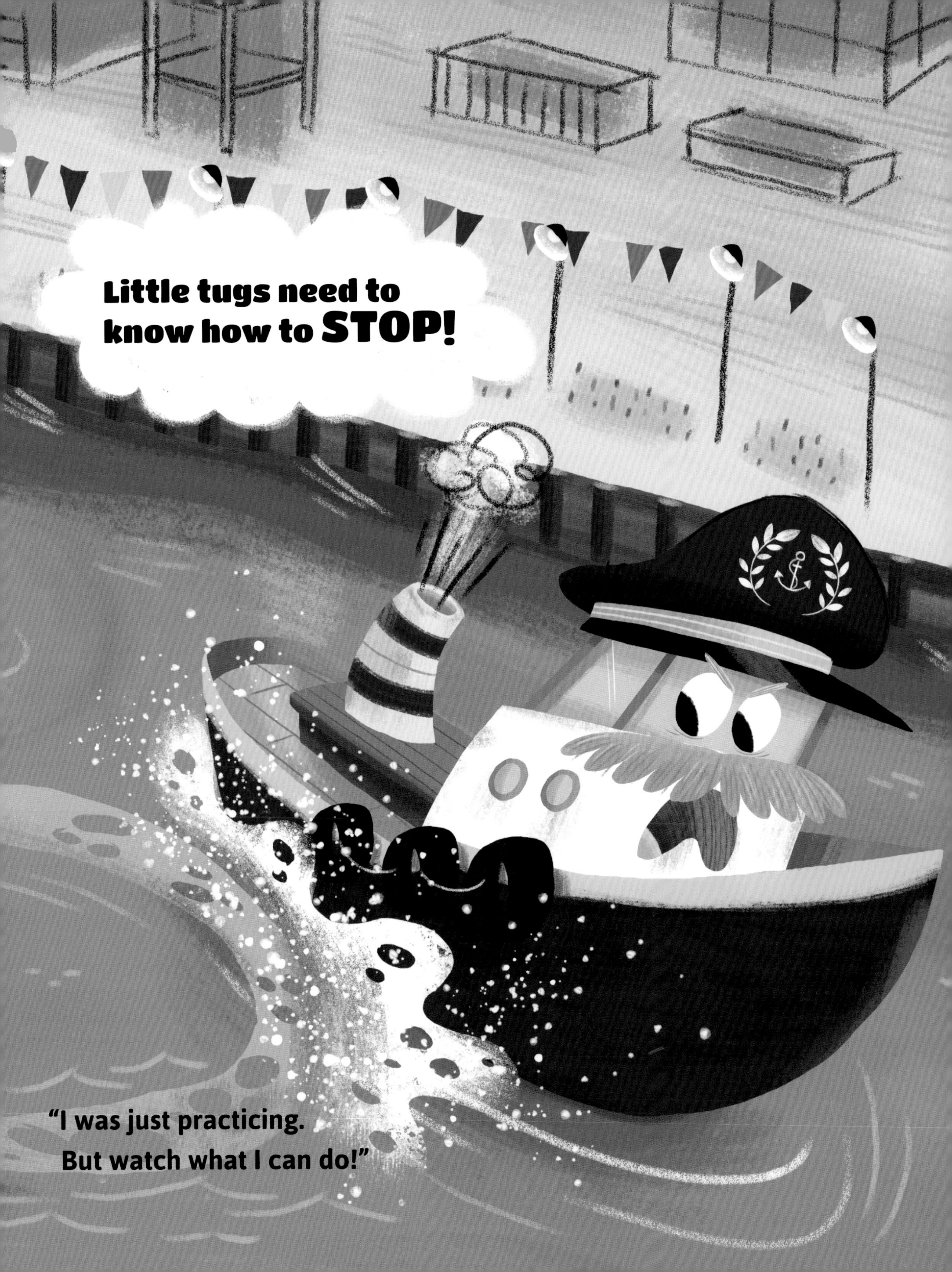

"I was just practicing.
But watch what I can do!"

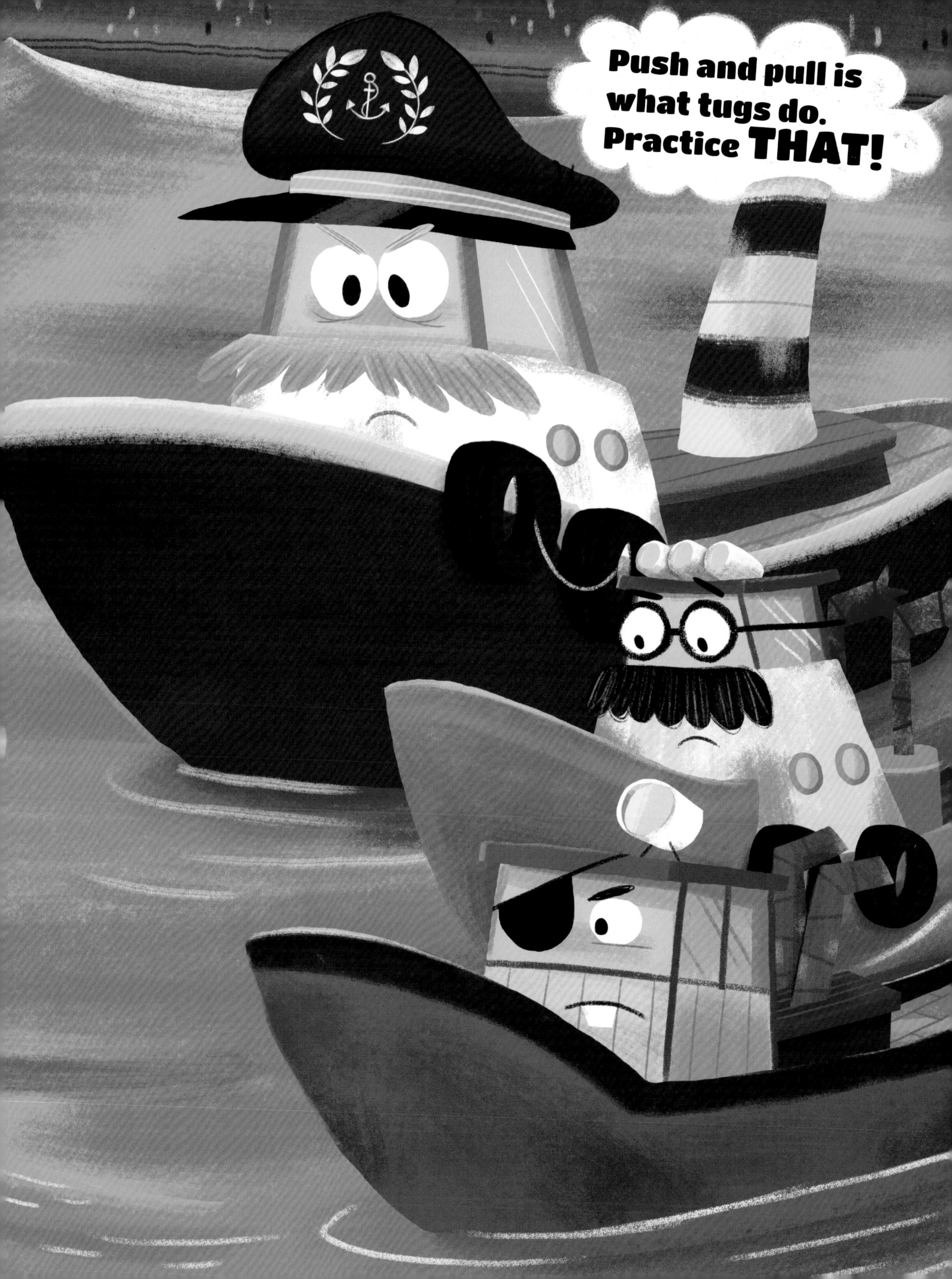
Push and pull is what tugs do. Practice THAT!

PUSH AND PULL.
PULL AND PUSH.

"Look, Barge! I'm pulling you!
I'll tow you to Alaska. My first job!"

READY, STEADY.
STEADY, READY.

"Being a tug sure is hard work.
But not too hard for me, 'cause I'm TOUGH TUG!"

CHUG AND TUG.

"Hey, Arctic Tug!
I'm going to Alaska too!
Want to race?"

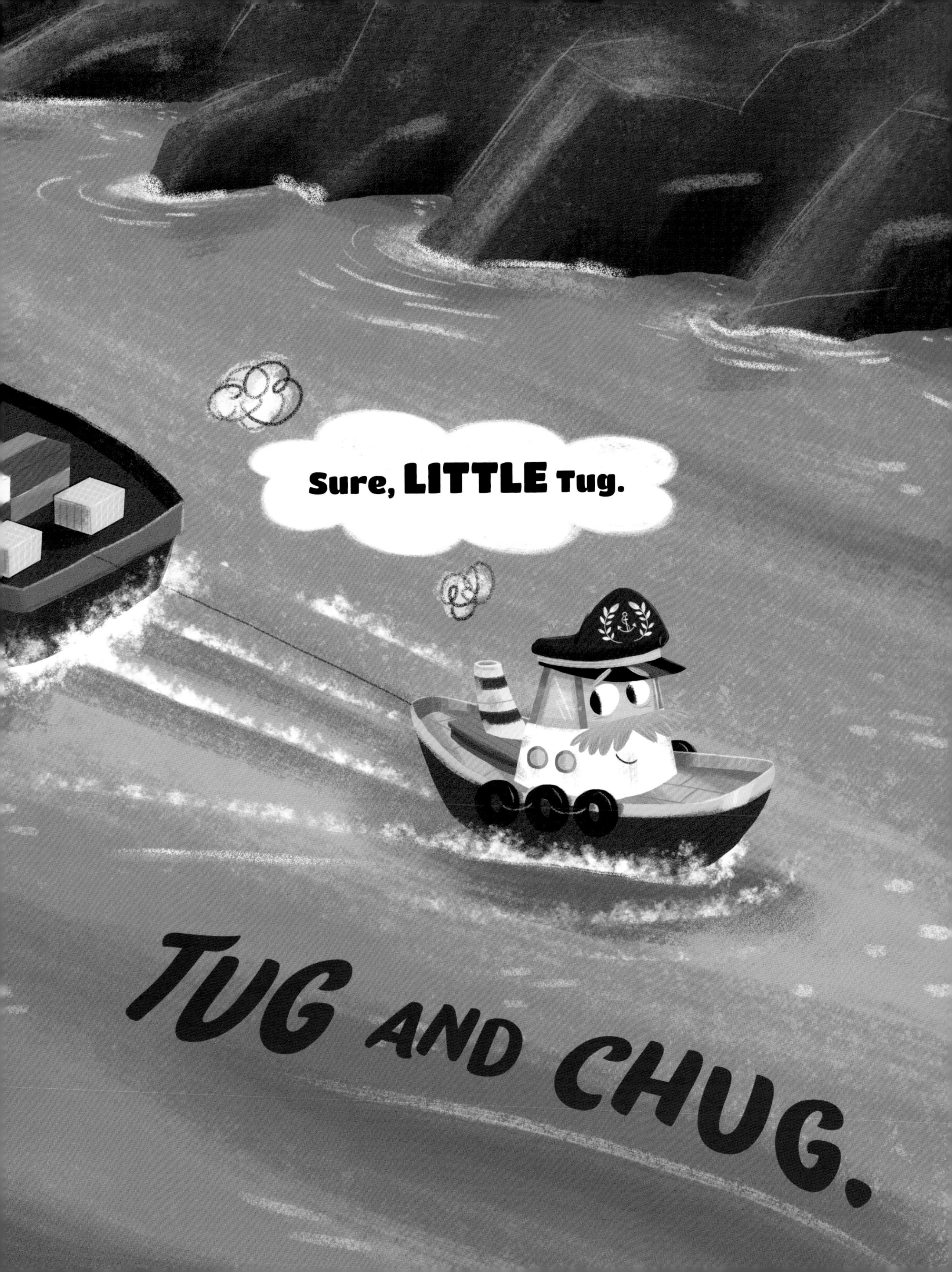
Sure, LITTLE Tug.
TUG AND CHUG.

RACE AND RUN! RUN AND RACE!

"I can catch you!
I'm Tough Tug!"

BYE-BYE, Little Tug.
Nice try! I'll see you in Sitka . . .
when you get there.

SLOW AND STOP.
SLOW AND STOP.

"You beat me to Alaska, Arctic Tug.
But still a long, long way to Anchorage.
And now we have to cross the open sea!"

"The open sea is rough.
Waves are high.
Wind is cold.
But I'm not worried.
I'm Tough Tug!"

"Arctic Tug lost power! Engine stopped!
I have to leave you, Barge. I've got to help.
I'll rescue Arctic Tug and come right back.
Don't worry. I can do this. I'm Tough Tug!"

HEAVY SEAS! HEAVY SEAS!

"Arctic Tug, I'll pull you.
I learned how!"

"It's hard to keep my course in heavy seas.
But I can do it. I'm Tough Tug!"

Thanks, Little Tug!
You towed me back to port!

SAFE AND SOUND.
SAFE AND SOUND.

"No problem, Arctic Tug!
A tugboat helps its friends!
Now back to pick up Barge. He's waiting for TOUGH TUG!"

"A long way back to port, Barge.
I know these waves are high.
But tough tugs don't give up.
And I'm your tug!"

ROCK AND REST.
ROCK AND REST.

Good job. You earned your name . . . **TOUGH TUG!**

"This trip was hard, but I did not give up. I left Barge safe in harbor. Now we rest.

"Another job tomorrow for . . . TOUGH TUG!"

For Murray Martin, our own Tough Tug.
And for his grandfather Thomas Martin, who manages tugboats!
–M.R.M.

For Bethany, Cassidy and Houston
–R.M.

———

Special thanks to my agent Alli, everyone at Two Lions, my critique group, and Keo for those late nights when I needed a fresh set of eyes on the page—R.M.

AUTHOR'S NOTE
This story is based on a true incident in which an Alaskan tug cut loose its own barge to rush to the rescue of the foundering tug of another tugboat company.

Published by Two Lions, New York

www.apub.com

Amazon, the Amazon logo, and Two Lions are trademarks of Amazon.com, Inc., or its affiliates.

ISBN-13: 9781503950986
ISBN-10: 1503950980

The illustrations are rendered in digital media.

Book design by Abby Dening
Printed in China

First Edition

1 3 5 7 9 10 8 6 4 2

ANCHORAGE, AK